A Drop of Rain

Wong Herbert Yee

Houghton Mifflin Company   Boston   1995

Library of Congress Cataloging-in-Publication Data

Yee, Wong Herbert.
    A drop of rain / by Wong Herbert Yee.
        p.   cm.
    Summary: Everyone in the family thinks that baby is crying and
tries to cheer him up until it is revealed that it is not tears but
drops of rain that are on baby's face.
    ISBN 0-395-71549-0
    [1. Babies—Fiction.   2. Rain and rainfall—Fiction.   3. Stories
in rhyme.]   I. Title.
PZ8.3.Y42Dr   1995   94-28676
[E]—dc20   CIP
                            AC

Printed in the United States of America

WOZ   10   9   8   7   6   5   4   3   2   1

To Matt, Kim, Katie, Nicole, Leslie, Erik,
Melissa, Christopher, Ellen, Alex and Adam
for reawakening the child in me.

A drop of rain fell from the sky,

And landed

    —PLOP!—

        in baby's eye.

"Why do you cry, sweetie pie?
A warm bottle will pacify."

As soon as Mother turned around,
Another drop of rain came down.
It trickled past the twigs somehow
And landed
    —SPLUNK!—
      on baby's brow.

"Why so glum, sugar plum?
A diaper change will sure help some."

As soon as Father turned around,
Another drop of rain came down.
It gathered where the gutters leak
And landed

   —*SPLAT!*—

      on baby's cheek.

"Why do you fret, precious pet?
Animal crackers you'll like, I bet."

As soon as Auntie turned around,

Another drop of rain came down.

It crawled along a climbing rose

And landed

    —PLUNK!—

        on baby's nose.

"Why so sad, lonesome lad?
A horsy ride will make you glad."

As soon as Uncle turned around,
Another drop of rain came down.
It traveled downward on its trip
and landed
   —*PLINK!*—
      on baby's lip.

"Why so dour, precious flower?
Perhaps a nap for half an hour."

As soon as Grandma turned around,
Another drop of rain came down.
It skipped off sister's violin
And landed
    —*SPLOT!*—
        on baby's chin.

"Why the frown, cuddly clown?
Let's take a buggy ride through town."

As soon as Grandpa turned around,
Another drop of rain came down.
It flicked off Grandpa's fishing gear
and landed

   —*SPLISH!*—

      in baby's ear.

"Why no joy for baby boy?
Sissy will bring your favorite toy."

As soon as Sister turned around,

Another drop of rain came down.

It splattered off the garden shed

And landed

    —SMACK!—

        on baby's head.

"What's the matter, little brother?
I'll hurry and go fetch Mother."

Brother found Mother
with a bottle in her hand

Baby took the bottle and
tossed it in the sand.

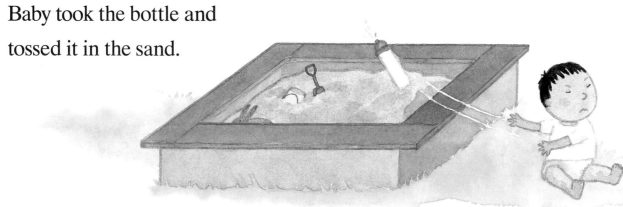

Father brought the diaper,
but baby was dry.

Auntie had crackers
that baby wouldn't try.

Uncle's horsy ride,
baby wouldn't take.

Grandma got the blanket,
but baby was wide awake.

Grandpa's buggy,
baby pushed away.

Sister found bunny,
but baby wouldn't play.

"There's nothing left to do," they sighed.

And everyone began to cry.

But then the morning sun burst through,
Changing the grey skies to blue.

As the clouds disappeared without a trace
A smile appeared on baby's face.